All Stuffe

Based on the episode "Dusty Bear"
by Sascha Paladino
for the series created by Chris Nee
Written by Catherine Hapka and adapted by Bill Scollon
Illustrated by Character Building Studio and
the Disney Storybook Art Team

BOOK FIVE

Disney PRESS

New York • Los Angeles

Doc and her toys Lambie and Stuffy are playing hide-and-seek. When Doc goes to find them in the closet, she notices something familiar.

It's a stuffed bear named Teddy B!

Teddy B used to be her brother, Donny's, favorite toy. They would go everywhere together!

"I bet Donny doesn't even know you're here," says Doc. "He's going to be so happy to see you!"

Doc takes Teddy B to Donny.

"I found something that's going to make you very happy," she tells him.

"Teddy B!" shouts Donny. "Wow, I've missed you so much."

But all of a sudden, Donny begins to sneeze. "Achoo, achoo–
ACHOO!" Poor Donny can't stop sneezing!

"I forgot this is why I can't play with him," Donny says glumly.

Doc takes Teddy B back to her room. As soon as they leave,
Donny stops sneezing.

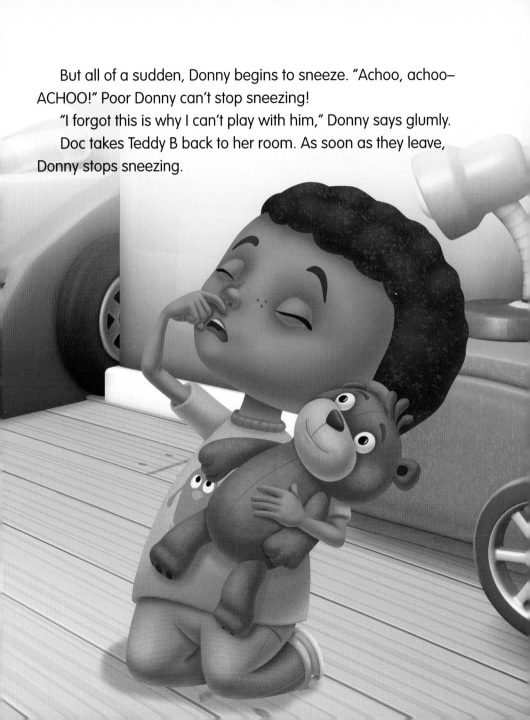

Doc has an idea. "Teddy, there's something about you that makes Donny sneeze. Let's see if we can find out what it is!"

Doc, Stuffy, and Lambie bring Teddy B to her clinic in the backyard. Hallie, Chilly, and Squeakers are there to greet them.

"Okay," says Doc. "It's time for your checkup!"

Doc listens to Teddy's heartbeat and checks his eyes and ears. Then she taps his knee with a rubber reflex hammer.

A cloud of dust flies into the air! Lambie and Stuffy start to cough.

"Wow, that is some dusty, dusty dust," says Lambie.

Doc has a diagnosis. She draws a picture in her Big Book of Boo-Boos.

"Teddy B has a bad case of the Dusty-Musties," she explains.

"What does that mean?" asks Teddy B.

"It means you're full of dust that's making Donny sneeze," Doc says. "He has allergies! All we have to do to cure you is to wash off the dust!"

Lambie and Stuffy follow Doc and Teddy B back into the house.

Doc asks her mom to help wash away Teddy's Dusty-Musties. Mom looks the bear over and agrees.

"I second your diagnosis," she says. "A good wash is just what this bear needs."

Doc and the toys wait by the washing machine while Mom goes to get a fresh bottle of laundry soap.

Teddy B looks at the big washing machine.
He's never been washed before.
"Are you ready for this?" Doc asks him.

"I'll do anything to be Donny's
toy again," he says. "But I am a little scared."
Lambie and Stuffy want to help.

Lambie has an idea. "What if we go in the washing machine with you?" she says.

Stuffy turns to Doc. "Can we?" he asks.

"Well, you both could use a wash," laughs Doc.

Doc puts the toys in the washer and gently closes the door. Teddy B feels much braver having his new friends come along with him.

Then Doc's mom puts in the laundry soap and pushes a button. "These guys will be clean in no time at all," she tells Doc.

Soon the toys are ready.

"That was fun!" says Teddy B. "And look at me. I'm clean! No dust!"

"Are you ready to see Donny?" asks Doc.

"Boy, am I," he answers.

Doc tells Donny about the Dusty-Musties. "But Teddy is cured," she says. "Now he won't make you sneeze."

Donny gives the bear a hug. His sister was right! "Thanks, Doc," he says.

Another toy cured! No more Dusty-Musties for Teddy B.
And Stuffy and Lambie feel clean and fresh, too!